The
Railway
Rabbits

Berry and the Amazing Maze

Georgie Adams

Illustrated by Anna Currey

Orion
Children's Books

First published in Great Britain in 2012
by Orion Children's Books
a division of the Orion Publishing Group Ltd
Orion House
5 Upper St Martin's Lane
London WC2H 9EA
An Hachette UK Company

1 3 5 7 9 10 8 6 4 2

Printed in Great Britain by Clays Ltd, St. Ives plc.

ISBN 978 1 4440 0258 4

www.orionbooks.co.uk
www.georgieadams.com

For Jasmine, Salima, and Bella, with love.
A.C

The Ripple River Valley

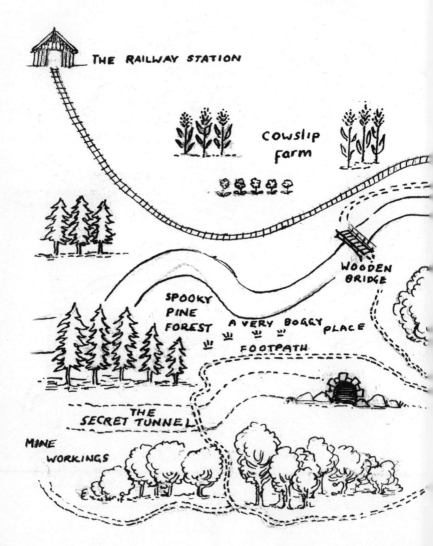

THE RAILWAY STATION

cowslip farm

WOODEN BRIDGE

SPOOKY PINE FOREST

A VERY BOGGY PLACE

FOOTPATH

THE SECRET TUNNEL

MINE WORKINGS

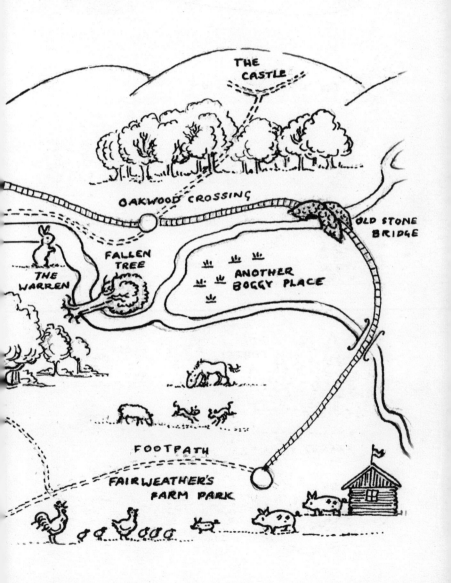

The Elders are Coming

1

At dawn one summer's day, the sun rose behind the castle on the hill, and birds sang to welcome the new day – the most special day of the year. It was the Gathering, a day when rabbits and friends met to feast and have fun under a harvest moon.

Barley and Mellow Longears woke early. Mellow went to wake her five young rabbits, who were fast asleep in cosy nooks tucked between the roots of a tree.

"Time to get up," said Mellow. "Your elders are coming. It's a special day, remember?"

"Marr!" said Bramble.

"It's too early." said Bracken.

"I'm sleepy," said Fern.

"I was dreaming," said Wisher.

Only Berry remembered about today. He opened his eyes wide and jumped out of his bed.

"Creeping caterpillars!" he said. "It's the Gathering! We're meeting our friends in a maize field at Fairweather's. Parr told us about it ages ago. He said there'd be lots of corncobs to eat. Mmm! We're going to have a moonlight feast."

The others gathered round excitedly.

"Of course!" said Bramble, cross with himself for not thinking of it first.

"We've been looking forward to the Gathering for such a long time," said Bracken.

"For EVER," said Fern.

"Not that long," said Wisher.

"There's lots to do before Elderparr Blackberry and Eldermarr Primrose arrive," said Mellow. "I need your help to clean and tidy the burrow."

Mellow found jobs for everyone, and soon they were all busy.

Barley tidied the tunnel entrance.

Bramble swept the floors.

Fern made a mat of wildflowers.

Bracken brushed the walls.

Wisher put herbs
in the hollows.

Mellow made sure everything was just
as it should be to welcome Blackberry
and Primrose to their home.

That morning, two elder rabbits, each grey about their ears and whiskers, hopped from their burrow, deep beneath the castle ruins. Blackberry and Primrose Longears were setting off to spend the Gathering with Barley Longears and his wife, Mellow, and their five young rabbits, Bramble, Bracken, Berry, Fern and Wisher. The elders were looking forward to seeing everyone again.

The two rabbits hopped downhill, stopping only to nibble a blade of grass or to sniff the air for an enemy.

Blackberry and Primrose knew how dangerous it was for them to be on the hill. The grass was short. There were few places to hide. A fox or a buzzard could strike at any moment!

Soon they reached Oak Wood where they felt safer, sheltered by trees and bushes. But it had been a long time since Blackberry and Primrose had been there. Everything looked different. Oak, beech and pines had grown into big, tall trees, and there were lots more paths than they remembered. Blackberry and Primrose didn't know which way to go. After a few wrong turns, and going round in circles, they found the right path and followed it through the wood.

From there, the elders went along
another path towards the River Ripple.
Barley and the others would be waiting
for them by the little wooden bridge.
The rabbits had arranged to meet at
midday, but the sun was already high in
the sky. They knew Barley would worry
his whiskers off if they were late, so
they hopped as fast as their legs could
carry them.

Barley looked at the sky. He checked to
see if their number one enemy Burdock
the buzzard was about. At the first sign
of trouble, Barley was ready to stamp
his hind foot on the ground three times
– thump, thump, thump! – the danger
signal the young rabbits knew so well.

To his relief, the bird was nowhere to
be seen. Then he noted the position of
the sun in the sky. He thought it must be
nearly midday.

"Ready?" he called back down the
tunnel to Mellow and the others. "It's time
to meet the elders."

First to appear were Bramble,
Bracken and Berry. They were followed
by Fern and Wisher, and last came
Mellow.

"Race you all to the bridge!" said
Berry. "Ready, steady – GO!"

The young rabbits dashed towards the
wooden bridge, while Barley and Mellow
hurried behind.

Bracken was the fastest, as usual, and
reached the bridge before everyone else.
He was disappointed to find the elders
hadn't yet arrived.

"We're a bit early," said Barley, glancing again at the sun.

"I'm sure Blackberry and Primrose will be here soon," said Mellow.

Berry hoped Marr was right. He was pleased his elders were coming to the Gathering too. It was going to be such fun. He was so excited he flipped a backwards somersault. It went a bit wrong and he nearly fell in the river.

"Oops!" said Berry.

The others laughed.

"Silly rabbit!" said Bramble.

While they waited, the young rabbits talked about their elders. It had been some time since Parr had first taken them to visit Blackberry and Primrose at Deep Burrow, under the castle ruins.

"It's where Fern found the silver hare, remember?" said Berry. "The one that once belonged to a princess."

Fern nodded.

"It reminded her of a real hare who danced on the hill," she said. "When the hare died the princess was very sad."

"She cried so much her tears made the River Ripple," said Wisher.

"Huh!" said Bramble. "It's only a story!" Bramble had always wished he'd been the one to find the silver hare, not Fern.

Seeing they might argue, Mellow said, "But it's a lovely story, isn't it? And the river is still flowing."

As they were talking, Barley paced up
and down, tugging his ears.

"My parents should have been here
by now," he said. "What if
something has happened?"

"Maybe they met a
fox?" said Fern. "Oh, Parr!
What if Elderparr and
Eldermarr have been
eaten? We'll never see
them again. They'll be
gone for EVER!"

"Oh, buttercups!"
said Barley.

The others were used to Fern
imagining the worst.

"We don't know anything of the sort,"
said Mellow. Then to calm everyone
down, she said, "Let's all sing something
cheerful."

Berry remembered a song Eldermarr
Primrose had taught them, and they all
joined in:

The River Ripple is its name,
Long may it gently flow.
So let us thank the hare who came
And danced so long ago.

They had just sung the last line when
Berry spotted Blackberry and Primrose
hurrying towards them.

"They've arrived!" he cried.

"Here we are!" said Primrose, hugging them all.

"Look how you've grown!" said Blackberry, beaming at the young rabbits.

"I'm still the smallest," said Wisher.

"Ah, but you have special powers," said Primrose. "It's a wonderful gift passed on by your great-great eldermarr, Meadow Silvercoat."

"Oh yes," said Blackberry. "Wisher is the one with tingly ears!"

Wisher's ears turned pink. She didn't understand why she was the only one in her family to hear voices inside her head or know things before they happened.

Barley was relieved to see his parents were safe and well.

"I was beginning to worry," he said.

"We thought you'd been eaten by a fox!" said Fern.

Primrose patted Fern's head. "Nothing quite so terrible," she said.

"We took a wrong turning or two in Oak Wood," said Blackberry.

"I remember getting lost when we visited you," said Barley.

"Yes, Parr," said Berry. "You took us round and round in circles!"

"My legs are tired from all that walking," said Primrose.

"Come and rest at the burrow," said Mellow. "There's plenty of time before we go to the Gathering tonight. And we have so much to talk about!"

Frights
at
Fairweather's
2

That afternoon, Fred Fairweather and
his helper, Jim, were busier than usual
at the Farm Park. A nosy ewe called Mrs
Woolly had been keeping her eye on
them. She liked to know everything that
went on around the farm, and today was
no exception.

She went to her friend, Agatha
Old Spot (proud mother of seven
beautiful piglets), to talk to her over
the pig sty wall.

"There's something going on I don't know about," said Mrs Woolly.

Agatha grunted. She was puzzled.

"If you don't know about it, Mrs Woolly," said Agatha, "how do you know it's going on?"

"Bah!" said Mrs Woolly. "I was just about to say. Fred and Jim have been hanging lanterns and putting up notices. They've cleared a pathway to the maize field too."

"Maize? What's that?" said Agatha.

"Corncobs," said Mrs Woolly.

"Yummy!" said Agatha.

"Fred sowed maize in the spring," said Mrs Woolly. "He's never grown it before. The plants are as tall as trees now. Well, maybe not quite so high. You can see them from here."

"My eyesight is not very good," said Agatha. "Are there any corncobs?"

"Yes," said Mrs Woolly. "Lots."

Just then, a large truck pulled into the farmyard. It was carrying the biggest, fiercest, strangest creatures Mrs Woolly had ever seen. For once in her life, she was speechless. Mrs Woolly stared and stared.

Sasha the sheepdog barked furiously
at the truck. She growled at the strange
creatures, but they took no notice. It was
as if they couldn't see or hear her.

"What's happening?" said Agatha
from her pig sty. "Is something wrong?"

Mrs Woolly was still in a daze.

"You're not going to believe this," she
said. Then she heard Fred give a shout:

"Open the maize field gate, Jim. The
dinosaurs are here!"

Agatha looked over the top of her sty.

"Dinosaurs?" she said. "What are they?"

"Those," said Mrs Woolly with a nod to the truck. "Fred has gone crazy. What is he thinking?"

Gilbert Goose and Hilda Hen came racing across the yard.

"Have you ever-ever-ever seen anything like it?" cried Gilbert, flapping his wings. "We're going to die-die-die!"

"He's right," said Hilda. "That creature with the long neck has a nasty look in its eye."

They all watched the truck as it
headed for the maize field.

"Now we know why Fred is growing
maize this year," said Mrs Woolly. "It's to
feed those maize-eating monsters!"

Agatha looked disappointed. "Oh,
dear!" she said. "I was looking forward
to having some."

"Really, Agatha!" said Mrs Woolly.
"Always thinking about your stomach.
There are more important matters on
my mind. We must find out about those
dinosaurs. I'd go myself but I'm stuck
behind this fence."

Hilda thought Mrs Woolly had been
a little unkind to Agatha, and she saw a
chance to get back at the bossy ewe.

"I'm Free Range," she said. "I can
roam wherever I please! I'll see what I
can do."

"I'll go with you," said Gilbert. He was afraid of the monsters, but Gilbert loved a good story! The arrival of the dinosaurs was the most exciting thing to happen at Fairweather's for a long time. He'd have something extra-specially-special to gossip about around the farm and along the riverbank. "Leave it to us," he said. "We'll take a sneaky-beaky look and report back."

Gilbert and Hilda hurried to the maize field. The gate was open, so they went in. The lorry was parked a little way inside the field. Gilbert and Hilda kept out of sight. It was easy for them to hide among the giant maize plants.

They looked so tall Hilda thought the
tops reached the sky. But what they saw
next took them both by surprise.

Fred and Jim were lifting the dinosaurs
down from the truck, one by one, and
carrying them along pathways through
the maize. Gilbert and Hilda followed
a little way behind, up one path and
down another.

They saw the men leave the creatures at various places in the maize. To Gilbert and Hilda's amazement, the monsters didn't move.

They didn't roar.

They didn't gnash their teeth.

They didn't growl.

They didn't blink
an eyelid!

"How wiggily-waggily-weird!"
whispered Gilbert in Hilda's ear.

"Maybe they're asleep?" said Hilda.

"Well, I don't want to be around when
they wake up!" said Gilbert. "I've seen
enough for one day. I'm off."

"Wait for me," said Hilda.

When they got back to the farmyard Gilbert and Hilda found Mrs Woolly waiting by the fence.

"Well?" she said. "Any news?"

"It's a bit puzzling," said Gilbert.

"Quite eggs-tra-ordinary," said Hilda.

"I'm all ears," said Mrs Woolly.

Off to the Gathering!

3

The grown-ups talked and talked. Barley, Mellow, Blackberry and Primrose lay in the sun, talking their tails off. Bramble, Bracken, Berry, Fern and Wisher soon got bored.

"Grown-ups!" said Berry. "They haven't stopped talking since Elderparr and Eldermarr got here. Oh, I can't wait to go to the Gathering."

"Tansy and Teasel will be there!" said Bramble.

"The twins?" said Bracken. "They're fun! We can play hide-and-seek in the maize."

"Parr says it's like a forest," said Fern.

"We might get lost," said Wisher.

"Even if we do," said Berry, "we won't be hungry. Think of all those lovely corncobs!"

The young rabbits tried to imagine what maize looked like. None of them had seen it before. They were all very excited. Berry looked back at the burrow. He could see Marr, Parr and the elders still deep in conversation.

"What do grown-ups find to talk about?" he said.

"I don't know," said Bracken.

"They'll be talking all afternoon," said Wisher.

"For EVER!" said Fern.

"Let's have a game of Tag-and-Tumble!" said Berry.

They played happily for a while, until Berry suddenly tripped on a tree-root. He fell into a prickly gorse bush.

"Creeping caterpillars!" cried Berry. "Ow, ooo, ouch!"

The others rushed to help.

"Here, give me your paw," said
Bramble, and pulled him up.

"Poor Berry!" said Bracken.

"You're covered in prickles!" said Fern.

"You look like a hedgehog!"
said Wisher.

"Very funny," said Berry.

Mellow, Barley, Blackberry and
Primrose came running to see what had
happened.

"Trust you, Berry!" said Mellow. "Stand
still while I remove the thorns. There.

All gone."

"Thanks, Marr,"
said Berry.

"You were so brave,
Berry," said Primrose.

"Accidents will
happen!" said
Blackberry cheerfully.

"Well, I hope there won't be any more," said Barley. "It's almost sunset. Time we were going to Fairweather's. The Gathering starts after dark."

"What are we waiting for?" cried Berry. "Come on!"

News of some strange goings-on at Fairweather's spread quickly along the riverbank. It began with Gilbert Goose who told his story to Daisy Duck.

"Oh, they were terrible-terrible-terrible," gabbled Gilbert. "Mrs Woolly thinks Fred has gone crazy. He's put a truck full of horrible-orrible-orrible monsters in the maize! Hilda Hen and I were there. We saw one as big as a barn! It had the longest neck you've ever seen in your life-life-life."

"Quack, quack, quack!" said Daisy. "What a dreadful tale!" She paddled away down river and the first friend she met was Violet Vole.

"Have you heard?" said Daisy.
"Mrs Woolly and Hilda Hen
have gone crazy! Fred put
them in a truck as big
as a barn. Gilbert
Goose has
grown a very
long neck and
some monsters are
eating the maize."

"How terrible!" said Violet.
"I must pass it on." She ran along the
riverbank and the first friend she met
was Sylvia Squirrel.

"Have you heard?" said Violet.
"Dreadful news! Don't know where to
begin. Trouble at Fairweather's, you see.
Hundreds of monsters have put Fred
in a truck and Gilbert Goose has gone
crazy eating maize. I think that's right?

Mrs Woolly has grown the longest neck you've ever seen, and Hilda Hen has grown as big as a barn!"

"Goodness," said Sylvia. "What a story! I must go and warn Barley and Mellow. I hear they're all going to Fairweather's tonight for the Gathering."

Sylvia Squirrel ran along the path. It wasn't long before she met the Longears family coming towards her. There were Barley and Mellow, Blackberry and Primrose, Bramble, Bracken, Berry, Fern and Wisher. The rabbits were singing happily as they walked:

"Hooray! Hooray! We're on our way,
We'll be at the Gathering soon.
To see our friends, to feast and play –
By the light of the harvest moon!"

They stopped when they saw Sylvia.

"Hello," said Barley. "Are you coming to the Gathering?"

"I was," said Sylvia, "until I met Violet Vole. She says there are some very strange goings-on at Fairweather's Farm Park."

Berry pricked his ears.

"What sort of things?" he said.

"Tell us," said Barley.

The rabbits crowded round to listen.

"Well," said Sylvia. "There are crazy, long-necked monsters loose in the maize. Hundreds of them, as big as barns!

They've eaten Fred and Mrs Woolly, would you believe? Fortunately, Gilbert Goose and Hilda Hen managed to escape in a truck to tell the tale."

Everyone's eyes were open wide. Berry couldn't believe his ears.

"WHAT?" he said.

"Oh, buttercups!" said Barley.

"Monsters?" said Bramble.

"Hundreds?" said Bracken and Fern together.

"Big as barns?" said Wisher.

"How dreadful," said Primrose.

"I've never heard anything like it," said Blackberry.

"Are you quite sure?" said Mellow.

"It's what I've been told," said Sylvia. "I shouldn't be surprised if every word of it were true."

Berry tried to make sense of Sylvia's fantastic story. He could see Parr tugging his ears and frowning.

"I don't know what to think," said Barley. "Even one monster would be terrible. We've enough to worry about with Burdock the buzzard, let alone a monster in the maize . . ."

Berry tried not to think the unthinkable, but he dared to ask the question that was whizzing inside his head.

"Parr," he said. "Are we still going to the Gathering?"

Five anxious young faces looked up at their parr, waiting for him to decide.

"Well . . ." said Barley.

At that moment, something caught Berry's attention. A shadow on the path – the shadow of a bird with outstretched wings. Berry thought he knew the shape of those enormous wings and who they belonged to. His heart thumped. He looked at the sky. There was no mistake. The hovering bird, dark against the glow of the setting sun, was every rabbit's worst enemy.

"Burdock!" cried Berry. "RUN!"

The buzzard dived.

The rabbits scattered in all directions.

The **Monster** in the **Maize**

4

Berry ran for his life. In his panic to escape from Burdock, he lost all sense of direction. He couldn't tell if he was heading for home or going the opposite way towards the farm. His only thought was to put as much distance between himself and the buzzard.

Fern was in front of him. She stopped
suddenly to catch her breath and Berry
caught her up. She was trembling
with fright.

"We must find somewhere to hide,"
said Berry.

"Oh, Berry! I'm glad you're here," said
Fern. "Do you think Marr and Parr and
everyone got away? What if Burdock—"

"Sssh!" said Berry. "Look, there he is!"

They looked up to see Burdock, his
wings outstretched, slowly circling in
the sky.

"Quick. Let's go or we're in trouble!"
said Berry.

Berry and Fern looked around.
Berry realised they had run towards
Fairweather's and had almost reached
the farm.

Not far away, they saw two long,
straight rails. Berry knew they were the
tracks of the Red Dragon – the monster
that roared along the valley every day,
whistling and belching clouds of smoke.

"Which way?" said Fern. "We mustn't
cross the tracks. The Red Dragon might
come along. Oh, Berry! We're trapped
between here and Burdock!"

But sharp-eyed Berry had just
spotted the very place to hide. It
was a field of tall, green plants.

"Follow me," he said.

A few minutes later, Berry and Fern crawled under a fence and slipped into a forest of maize.

Twilight was falling as Berry and Fern hopped along a narrow pathway through the maize. There were corncobs everywhere, and a few had fallen from their stems. Golden corncobs lay on the ground – ripe and ready to eat.

Berry loved corncobs, but he didn't feel like eating. He was too scared! His heart was beating fast. At any moment they could be spotted by Burdock. He wished Marr and Parr and the others were here. "How much further?" said Fern. "Haven't we gone far enough?"

"The maize looks thicker over there," said Berry, who was leading the way. "We'll stop then and think what to do."

"What about the m-m-monsters?" said Fern. Ever since they'd discovered the maize field, Fern had been nervous. She remembered every word of Sylvia Squirrel's tale about crazy monsters as big as barns.

"It was probably just a story," said Berry, sounding braver than he felt. He didn't want to let Fern know he was scared or that he was afraid they'd meet a beast at any moment. He wished Bramble was here. Bramble was brave. He'd know what to do!

They were turning a corner when they heard voices nearby. Berry and Fern stopped in their tracks. Then they dived into the maize to listen.

"Where is everybody?" said a young rabbit's voice.

"Are you sure we're in the right field, Marr?" said another.

"Yes, Tansy," said the marr rabbit. "Mellow said we should meet in the maize. I wonder where they are, Lop?"

"I expect Barley has lost his way, Lilly," said the one called Lop. "Trust good old Barley Longears!"

By now, Berry and Fern knew just who they were. They came out of hiding and ran to greet them. When Tansy and Teasel saw Berry and Fern they waved excitedly. The twins looked exactly the same. They both had grey fur and their paws and tummies were white. But Berry remembered that Tansy had straight ears, and her brother's were floppy.

"Hi, Tansy!" said Berry.

"Hi, Teasel!" said Fern.

"Great to see you," said Tansy.

"Where are Bramble, Bracken and Wisher?" said Teasel. The twins' parents, Lop and Lilly Greyback, came over.

"Where are Barley and Mellow?" said Lilly, looking around.

Berry told her how they'd all had to run from Burdock.

"Oh dear!" said Lilly.

"I'm sure they'll be fine," said Lop. "Barley is a clever rabbit! They'll be along for the Gathering soon."

They waited and waited, but there was no sign of Barley and the rest of the family. Berry was sure something dreadful must have happened, but he kept his fears to himself. He didn't want to appear silly or make a fuss in front of his friends.

"Let's play hide-and-seek," said Tansy.

"Good idea," said Teasel.

"I'm not sure . . ." said Berry. "Maybe we should wait for the others?"

"We might meet a monster!" said Fern.

Tansy and Teasel looked surprised.

"What monster?" they said together.

Berry told them Sylvia's story. "Hm!" said Tansy. "I think it's just a made-up story. If there were hundreds of monsters as big as barns here, we'd have seen one by now."

"Tansy's right," said Teasel.

"Thank you," said Tansy. "I usually am."

"Okay," said Berry. "Let's play until the others come."

Fern decided to join in. She didn't want Tansy and Teasel to think she was being scared for nothing.

"Don't go too far," said Lilly. "It'll be dark soon."

"We don't want anyone to get lost!" said Lop.

"You hide first," Berry said to the others. "I'll count to twenty." He put his paws over his eyes and started counting. "One, two, three . . ."

Berry had just reached "eighteen" when he heard a shriek – a chilling, high-pitched cry. Then: "Berry! Berry! Help!" It was Fern.

"Coming, Fern!" cried Berry. "I'm coming!"

Berry raced through the maize, which stood on either side of him like thick hedges. Berry couldn't see a thing between the stems.

Then he heard Fern cry out again, closer than before.

"Fern!" he called. "Where are you?"

There was no reply. The only sound he could hear was the wind blowing through the maize and rustling the leaves. He ran towards the sound – towards where he hoped to find Fern. But there were so many twists, turns and pathways that Berry began to panic.

"I'll never find her in this forest!" he said. Rounding a corner, he suddenly came to a clearing. Then he stopped. The biggest, fiercest creature Berry had ever seen was blocking his way. The monster was ENORMOUS!

Berry thought its body must be as high
as a hill. It had a huge horn on its nose
and sharp spikes along its back. He had
never in all his life seen anything like it.

Berry opened his mouth to cry out, but nothing came. His throat was dry. He was shaking with fright. When he dared take his eyes off the monster for a few seconds, Berry looked around the clearing for Fern. She was nowhere to be seen.

Berry
Braves
the
Beasts
5

Berry had no idea how long he stood
staring at the monster. He couldn't speak.
He couldn't move. His paws were stuck
to the ground. But thoughts buzzed
inside his head like bees. Sylvia was
right. There are monsters! Where is Fern?
I wonder what's happened? Has the
monster has eaten her? I'll never see
Fern again. Creeping caterpillars! It
might eat me too!

Tansy and Teasel appeared
behind him.

"Berry," said Tansy, and stopped.

She couldn't believe what she
was seeing.

Teasel got such a fright his floppy ears
stood straight up on top of his head.

"Don't say a word," Berry whispered.
With his eyes fixed on the monster, he
took a small step back. Slowly, he
took another and another, until he was
with Tansy and Teasel. Then he said:
"Let's . . . GET OUT OF HERE!"

Berry, Tansy and Teasel ran. They darted this way and that, flew down one path and raced along another. They didn't stop until they reached the edge of the field. Lop and Lilly were anxiously waiting for them.

"We heard some shouts," said Lilly.

"Is everything all right?" said Lop.

"No," said Berry. "It isn't."

Fred Fairweather was getting ready for visitors to arrive at the Farm Park. Earlier, while he'd been feeding the animals, Fred had stopped to tell Mrs Woolly what was happening.

Fred believed in talking to his animals, which suited Mrs Woolly very well. She now knew exactly what was going on, and couldn't wait tell everyone else!

As Fred waited for the steam train to arrive at Fairweather's Halt – the train was bringing visitors to his special attraction – Mrs Woolly told Gilbert Goose, Hilda Hen and Agatha Old Spot everything she knew.

"It's really very funny," said Mrs
Woolly. "Those dinosaurs we saw this
afternoon aren't real. They're, er, what
did Fred call them? In-flabber-balls.
In-flatter-bulls . . ."

"Do you mean inflatables?" said Hilda.

"Thank you," said Mrs Woolly,
though she was annoyed with herself
for not getting the word quite right.
"The dinosaurs inflate. They blow up
like balloons, you see? They're quite
harmless. Nothing to worry about at all."

"I wish we'd known that earlier," said
Hilda. "They looked real enough when
Gilbert and I saw them close up."

"True," said Gilbert. "But we
wondered why they didn't move."

"We thought they were asleep!"
said Hilda.

"Why does Fred want un-flappable dinosaurs or whatever they're called?" said Agatha, trying her best to keep up.

"I was just coming to that," said Mrs Woolly. "Fred has made an Amazing Maze in the maize field."

Agatha looked very confused. "I'm getting in a muddle with all these mazes!" she said.

"A maze is a people thing," said Mrs Woolly. "People-folk go round and round in it getting lost, before they find their way out! Fred has put inflatable

dinosaurs in his maze and called it
Dinosaurs in the Dark. People-folk will
bring torches and have fun in it tonight."

"Hm?" said Agatha, scratching her ear.
"It doesn't sound much fun to me."

Just then, they heard a loud whistle.

Whooo-Wheeep!

"There's the train," said Mrs Woolly.
"The visitors have arrived!"

"I don't know what to think," said Lilly
when Berry, Tansy and Teasel had told
them about Fern, and about seeing an
enormous monster in the maize.

She was used to her naughty twins
getting up to mischief. Tansy had a wild
imagination and was good at making up
stories. "Though I am worried about Fern.
I expect she's still playing hide-and-seek
and waiting for Berry to find her. But it's
getting dark . . ."

"Well, I don't believe a word about the
monster!" said Lop.

"Parr!" said the twins together.

"It's true," said Berry. "And about Fern."

Lop smiled. "I think you're all having a little joke," he said. "You're excited. After all, it is the Gathering. But Lilly is right about Fern. She should be here by now."

"I'll go and find her," said Berry. He could see it was useless trying to persuade the grown-ups Fern was missing and in real danger. Before anyone could stop him, Berry ran back into the maize.

As night fell, the harvest moon rose like a golden ball in a starry sky. Gentle moonbeams lit Berry's way as he went along the paths, calling and calling to Fern. He felt frightened and very alone. So much had happened since they'd been attacked by Burdock. That buzzard had spoiled everything! Where were Marr and Parr? Had Bramble, Bracken and Wisher got away? Were Elderparr Blackberry and Eldermarr Primrose okay? And now Fern was missing! Oh, I wish Marr and Parr were here, he thought. They'd know what to do . . .

The sudden shriek of a whistle interrupted his thoughts.

Whooo-Wheeep!

"The Red Dragon!" said Berry. "That's strange. He doesn't usually come out at night."

The Red Dragon's tracks passed close by the maize field. Berry could hear him rattling and clattering along his rails – Clickerty-clack. Clickerty-click – and puff-puff-puffing smoke. Other sounds came to Berry's pricked ears – a slow, chug-chug-chugging, a long squeal, the hiss! of hot, steamy breath. Then silence. Berry could tell the Red Dragon had stopped.

By now Berry had almost given up hope of finding Fern. His throat was sore from calling her name, but he tried again.

"Fern!" he called. "Fern! It's me, Berry. Where are you?"

Berry only half-expected a reply. He was afraid Fern had been eaten by the enormous monster he'd seen earlier. A second or two passed. Berry pricked his ears. He was startled by the sudden snap! of a dry twig. Then he heard leaves rustling nearby. What was that? Oh, I hope it's not another scary beast! To his relief, he saw a small rabbit with soft-grey fur pushing her way through the maize.

"Fern!" cried Berry.

"I've been so frightened," said Fern, running to Berry. "I saw this t-t-t-terrible m-m-m-monster and ran away. I'm not making it up, Berry. It was the scariest beast EVER!"

"It's okay," said Berry. "I believe you."

"Really?" said Fern.

"Yes," said Berry. "I saw it too. So did Tansy and Teasel. We thought . . . oh, never mind. You're safe! That's all that matters. Come on. We've all been so worried about you."

Berry and Fern were about to leave when they heard the footsteps.

Thud, thud, thud!

The rabbits felt the ground vibrate. Something heavy was pounding down the path behind them. Thud, thud, thud!

They crouched in the darkness, their hearts thumping.

"Wh-wh-what is it?" said Fern.

Berry gulped. "I don't know," he said. "But it's coming our way. Fast!"

Terrified of what they might see, Berry and Fern turned. They were dazzled by a beam of light and froze in its glare.

"It's the monster!" said Fern. "We'll never see Marr and Parr, Bramble, Bracken and Wisher again!"

"Oh, help!" said Berry.

They shut their eyes and waited for their fate.

A Moonlight Feast

6

Meanwhile, Barley and his family were slowly making their way along the riverbank towards Fairweather's.

It had taken some time for everyone to find each other again after they'd run from Burdock. Everyone, that is, except Berry and Fern. Barley and Mellow, the elders Blackberry and Primrose, Bramble, Bracken and Wisher were keeping a lookout for the missing rabbits.

"Oh, I hope they're all right," Mellow kept saying as they went along.

"I'm worried too," said Barley. "There's no sign of them yet. I hope we're going the right way, Bramble?"

"I saw them running towards Fairweather's, Parr," said Bramble, who was leading the way. "Look. We're nearly there."

"Fern was so scared," said Bracken.

"We were all scared," said Wisher. She was walking a little way behind the others with her elders.

"That buzzard!" said Blackberry crossly.

"We never have a moment's peace with that bird around!" said Primrose. A few minutes later, Wisher stopped. She had a faraway look in her eyes.

"What is it?" said Primrose.

"It's my ears, Eldermarr," said Wisher. "They started to tingle when we were talking about Berry and Fern just now. I can hear a voice inside my head."

"What does it say?" said Mellow. She hoped Wisher's special powers might help them find Berry and Fern. Wisher told them:

Wisher, beware. Wisher, take care!
Berry's in danger. Fern's had a scare.
Where patterns of pathways confuse and amaze,
In a forest of green – they're lost in a maze!

"Patterns of pathways?" said Mellow.

"What's a maze?" said Bracken. "And where is the forest of green?" said Barley.

Wisher's eyes opened wide. "Don't you remember, Parr?" she said. "When you told us about the Gathering, you said the maize was like a forest."

"So I did!" said Barley.

Bramble pointed to a field not
far away.

"There it is!" he said.

"I can see Tansy and Teasel," said
Wisher excitedly. "Lop and Lily are
with them."

"Race you to the gate," said Bracken
to Bramble and Wisher.

"Stay where I can see you," said
Mellow. "Remember: Sensible rabbits
have careful habits! I don't want anyone
else to go missing!"

"People-folk!" said Berry and Fern.

The young rabbits were sitting on
a path in the maize gazing after two
children who had just run by carrying
sticks of bright light.

Their footsteps shook the ground and it sounded very frightening. Nearby, Berry and Fern could hear excited shrieks and yells.

"There are lots of people-folk here," whispered Berry nervously.

"What are they doing?" said Fern.

"I don't know," said Berry. "Maybe they're hunting m-m-monsters?"

A flash of yellow suddenly swept across their path and for a split-second the rabbits were caught in its glare.

The beam moved on. Then they heard a scream.

"Ooo!" said Fern. "I think they've found one. I'm scared, Berry. What if they don't catch him? What if the monster eats them up? If we're caught, he'll eat us too!"

"You're right," said Berry. "Let's go. We must find the others as fast as we can. They'll be very worried."

They set off along a path, hoping they were going in the right direction. There were so many paths through the maize it was difficult to know where they were. Luckily for the rabbits, the harvest moon had risen high in the sky and its beams were lighting their way. Every now and then, they heard people-folk calling to one another in the maize, which the rabbits found strangely comforting.

"I'd rather meet people-folk than monsters!" said Berry.

"Well, I hope we don't meet either," said Fern. "Some people-folk eat rabbits, remember? They put them in a pie!"

They had just reached the end of a path, which had brought them to the edge of the field when . . .

"BOO!"

Berry and Fern nearly jumped out of
their skins. "Found you!" said Bramble,
Bracken Wisher, Tansy and Teasel.

Berry was amazed to discover that while
they had been lost in the maize, a large
number of their family and friends had
arrived for the Gathering. Berry's eyes
opened wide at the sight of so many
waiting to greet them.

"Hooray!" cheered the crowd.

Mellow hugged Berry and Fern tightly.

Everyone was relieved to see them safe and well. Now they were all together again the celebrations could begin.

"Well," said Barley. "I don't know about anyone else but I'm hungry. Look at all these corncobs! Let's begin the feast. And while we're eating, Berry and Fern can tell us what happened."

Lop and Lilly exchanged knowing glances with Barley and Mellow.

"It's quite a story," said Lop.
"Scary too!"

"Yes," said Lilly. "Apparently there's
a terrible monster in the maize!"

After all that had happened, Berry
had to make the grown-ups believe his
story was true.

"THERE IS!" he cried. "It's the scariest
thing I've seen in my life. It's enormous."

"The biggest EVER!" said Fern.

"With a horn on its nose," said Tansy.

"And spikes down its back,"
said Teasel.

"Wriggly worms!" said Bramble.

"Slugs and snails!" said Bracken.

"Buzzy bees!" said Wisher.

"There!" said Sylvia Squirrel. "What did I tell you, Barley? The rumours were true. There are hundreds of monsters around here. I shouldn't be surprised if we're not eaten alive! I should never have come . . ."

Just then, everyone heard a scream.

"Oh, buttercups!" said Barley.

"Oh my stars!" said Mellow. "Look."

Berry gasped. "It's another monster," he said.

"I don't feel very well," said Barley.

"I must be seeing things," said Lop.

"We've eaten too much maize," said Lilly.

"Now do you believe me?" said Berry.

Lop and Lilly nodded. They were much too frightened to speak.

At that very moment, Gilbert Goose and Hilda Hen arrived. They had heard about the Gathering and had come to join in the fun.

"Having a nice time?" said Gilbert, eyeing a pile of half-eaten maize.

"Mmm!" said Hilda. "Corncobs are my favourite!"

Barley pointed to the monster. "How can you even think of eating with that c-c-creature about?" he said.

"Oh, that," said Hilda. "Don't you know? It's a dinosaur. Wouldn't hurt a fly!"

"It's an inflatable dinosaur," said Gilbert. He told everyone about Fred Fairweather's Amazing Maze.

"Well, I never!" said Barley when Gilbert had finished.

"Creeping caterpillars!" said Berry.

Later that night, a long procession of animals slowly made their way home to burrows, dens and nests along the riverbank and beyond. Everyone agreed it had been the best Gathering they could remember.

"I'll never forget tonight, Marr," Berry said as he walked along with Mellow.

"It was full of surprises!" said Mellow. "I'm glad those dinosaurs weren't real. It's strange what people-folk do to amuse themselves, isn't it? Scaring themselves in the dark and getting lost in a maize maze!"

"It wasn't funny," said Berry, remembering how afraid he had been.

"I was so scared," said Fern.

"You were very brave, Berry," said Bramble. "Going to look for Fern with those monsters about."

"Yes," said Bracken. "Berry the Brave!"

"It was nothing," said Berry, but he was pleased to know they were proud of him. "How did you know where to find us?"

"My ears," said Wisher. "I heard voices. You know . . ."

Just then, the Red Dragon came along – *clickerty-click, clickerty-clack!* – on his way home. There were lights along his back, and people-folk waving to the animals.

"There's another strange thing people-folk do," said Barley. "I'll never understand why they ride the Red Dragon. He's a real monster!"

The Red Dragon puffed smoke into the starry sky and gave the rabbits a cheery whistle as he went by:

Whooo-Wheeep!

Bramble, Bracken, Berry, Fern and Wisher waved. Wisher's special friend, Parsley Mole, was there too.

"He's all huff, puff and smoke that one," said Parsley.

"Not such a monster after all," said Wisher.

Back at the burrow, five tired but happy young rabbits curled up in their nests.

After his extraordinary day, Berry couldn't quite believe he was home where he felt safe and warm, surrounded by the family he loved.

His marr gave him a cuddle and whispered: "Brave Berry!"

Barley smiled. "I'm proud of you too, Berry," he said.

Then they kissed them all goodnight.

"Goodnight, Bramble."

"Goodnight, Berry."

"Goodnight, Bracken."

"Goodnight, Fern."

"Goodnight, Wisher."

"Goodnight, little rabbits. Sleep well!"

Author's Note

The Kensey Valley in North Cornwall where I live, and the Launceston Steam Railway inspired the location of The Railway Rabbits. The route of the railway along this unspoilt river valley provided me with the perfect setting for these stories – and all within walking distance of my cottage.

One morning in January 2010 I went to see the owners of the railway, Kay and Nigel Bowman. Sitting in the Station Café they told me how their railway worked, and some of the weird and wonderful things they'd seen whilst driving the trains. Yes, Kay is a train driver too! I based my idea for Wisher and the Runaway Piglet on a real pig that found its way on to the track. I even got to ride on the footplate of a red locomotive called Covertcoat, which was my inspiration for the Red Dragon.

The stories are told mostly from the rabbits' point of view and, from this perspective, these are big adventures for little rabbits. I've tried to convey a sense of reality about the dangers rabbits face living in the wild – the Longears' number one enemy is Burdock the buzzard. I often see these magnificent birds circling over our valley, and there's usually one sitting on a telegraph pole near my cottage.

I hope you enjoy reading all the books in this series as much as I've enjoyed writing them. A big thank you to everyone at Orion Children's Books – they are simply the best. Special thanks go to my publisher, Fiona Kennedy; my editor, Jenny Glencross; designers Loulou Clark and Abi Hartshorne and to Anna Currey for her wonderful illustrations.   Happy reading!

Georgie Adams
Cornwall, 2012